Are You Kidding?

by

Bali Rai

First published in 2008 in Great Britain by
Barrington Stoke Ltd
18 Walker Street, Edinburgh, EH3 7LP

www.barringtonstoke.co.uk

ISBN: 978-1-84299-540-2

Printed in Great Britain by Bell & Bain Ltd

A Note from the Author

When I wrote *Two-Timer*, I never dreamt that it would be the first of three books about Marcus, Dal, Kully and the rest of the crew! But I'm very pleased that it was. You see, once the goat, Flossie, entered the first story, there was just no turning back. And after so many questions about exactly *why* there was a goat in the first two books, I just had to explain.

So – after a lot of thinking, planning and a load of stupid research into goats (I didn't even need it!) – here's why. Enjoy this book *and* find out Flossie's fate! At last.

Contents

Chapter 1
Surprise

"What surprise? What are you talking about?" I asked my dad.

It was 7.30 on a Monday morning and my dad was in the bathroom having a shave. He'd just told me I'd have a nice surprise when I got to school that morning.

"How's it a surprise if I tell you, Marcus?"

"Dad ..."

"I'm trying to shave, son ..."

I watched him finish shaving his chin. Then he started putting shaving foam on his head. He's always had a shaved head and sometimes he cuts it when he shaves. He sticks tissue to the cuts to soak up the blood. It looks well stupid.

"Marcus, go and get ready for school before I kick your ass for you ..." Dad said.

"Easy, baldy, no need to get stressed," I said with a grin. "You giving me a lift?"

He nodded.

"Cool. We can pick Harj up on the way."

I went downstairs and made myself some toast. My sister, Teesha, was downstairs too. She was reading some stupid magazine.

"Which Hollywood star is on a diet now?" I asked her.

"Shut up," she said. She didn't even look up from the story she was reading.

Teesha is 18 and works in town as a hairdresser. And we don't get on at all.

"Should be a picture of you in there," I said.

"'Cos I look like a star?" she asked.

"Nah," I shook my head. "'Cos you look like you could do with one of them diets."

This time she threw the magazine down on the table and got up.

"You stupid idiot ..."

That was as far as she got before Mum walked in.

"Stop it – both of you!"

Teesha thought about moaning about me but it was no good. Mum was like one of them statues. Solid and unbending.

"Dad says I've got some surprise happenin' at school an' that," I told Mum. "You know what it is?"

She nodded.

"*And* ...?" I needed to know.

"*And* eat your toast and drink your juice and mind your business," she replied. "And can you explain why your football kit looks like it was dragged through a mud pit by a herd of elephants?"

"It weren't that bad," I protested.

"The mud that came off it blocked the waste pipe, Marcus," she added. "Your dad had to take the pipe to bits and clean it out ..."

"It was raining. So I got muddy," I said. That was a lie, but I wasn't going to tell her that me and Harj had been skidding in these big puddles, was I? That would have been stupid.

"Is your dad giving you a lift?" she asked me.

"Yeah ... better go," I said.

"Be good," she told me. "And enjoy your surprise ..."

****

At school, our form teacher, Miss Bramley, told us we had to go to a special Assembly.

"The entire school will be at this Assembly so it'll be a squeeze ..." she said.

"Like in your bra, miss?" asked Harj, so soft that Miss Bramley wouldn't hear.

Miss Bramley didn't hear. She carried on.

"... it'll only take ten minutes so that should be fine," she said.

"Thanks, miss," whispered Harj. "But it won't take that long ..."

"But we only go to Assemblies on Thursdays, innit?" shouted a lad called Steve.

"No," said Miss Bramley. She looked stern. "You go when you get told to go."

Steve went red and shut up as Miss Bramley went on talking about some other stuff. She was really pretty and had one of them footballers' wives' figures – all curves and that. All the lads fancied her and Steve was gutted that he'd got told off by her. Harj told him so.

"Shut up, fool," grunted Steve.

"Better a fool than a loser," Harj added.

"Better a loser than a ... a ..." Steve said, but he ran out of words.

"Done yer!" said Harj.

"Something to tell me, Harj?" asked Miss Bramley.

"He wishes, miss," shouted Lucy, one of the girls. Everyone started to laugh and Miss Bramley joined in. And, I swear, she winked at me as she did. Serious ...

Mr Brimstone took the Assembly. He was a deputy head and a Biology teacher. It was in the main hall and it stank of bleach and cleaning in there. A month ago, just before the Christmas holidays, there'd been a little accident in the hall, to do with loads and loads of goat poo. Me and Harj had helped with the 'accident' so we grinned at each other as we entered. But what had happened is a different story ...

Our class was the last to arrive and Mr Brimstone waited for us. The hall was packed and I ended up standing right up against a girl called Mina Patel.

"You mind?" she said, as I got pushed up next to her.

"Nope," I said, with a smile.

"Stupid jerk," she said but she was smiling too. My mind started to wander. Well, maybe just my eyes ...

7

"SILENCE!" boomed Mr Brimstone. His voice was so loud that it rang out round the hall.

"Man, he's loud," I whispered to Mina.

"And you're too fresh," she said as she pushed my hands away from her hips.

Oh – didn't I tell you that I'd done that? Silly me.

"As you all know, the new school library will be opened in two weeks' time by the Lord Mayor. Of course, as you'd expect, the school will be putting on a show and there will be a lot of media attention. All the local newspapers will be here, and local TV and radio. It will be down to you pupils to get involved and make sure that everything goes smoothly. Because of that, and because I know that some of you find good behaviour difficult, we're going to split the school up. Some of you will be at the opening. Most of you won't. Your teachers will sort that out this week ..."

He coughed.

"I've also got two other items of news. As of today we have a new school mascot ..."

Everyone stared as the doors behind Mr Brimstone opened and another teacher, Mr Simms, walked in. Behind him was a big grey goat.

"*Loser!*" shouted one of the pupils. It sounded like Harj's cousin Kully.

"Who said that?" screeched Mrs Pincher, the head.

When no one owned up, she went red.

"That's just the sort of behaviour we won't tolerate at the Grand Opening," warned Brimstone as Mr Simms dragged the goat to the front of the hall.

"This is Flossie," said Brimstone. "Some of you may have seen her around the school over the past few months. Well, we have now adopted her and she'll be our mascot."

I looked around at the faces of my fellow pupils. Everyone was just standing staring at the goat. In shock.

"We're gonna get ripped over this," said a lad in Year Eleven. "What will all the other schools say?"

"Just imagine what them dick-heads at City are gonna say," added his mate. City School was across town and they hated us like we hated them.

"Silence!" shouted Mr Brimstone.

When there was silence, he went on.

"The second piece of news is that we have a new caretaker for the school. I expect you can all remember the terrible thing that happened to Mr Spencer ..."

Mr Spencer had been our old caretaker but he'd left now. He'd been fixing a broken toilet when all the water just poured out everywhere. The soil pipe fell off and the water spilled all over the boys' toilets and Mr Spencer slipped and fell and twisted his ankle. He wouldn't come back to work after that. That's what my dad said, anyway. I was thinking about his accident and Flossie the goat when the surprise my parents had told me about walked into the hall.

"Well, pupils, I'd like you to meet Mr Delgado." Mr Brimstone boomed.

This time my jaw hit the floor.

"Hey, Marcus," said Harj. "Ain't that your grandad?"

I nodded.

Chapter 2
Revenge

Now I know it shouldn't be a big deal. But having my gramps working at school was a nightmare. I'd been at the school for four years and I knew the way the pupils treated caretakers. Plus my gramps had a really strong Jamaican accent. I could just see the other kids making fun of him.

Just two days after the Assembly, me and Harj were walking to History when I heard my gramps shouting to me.

"YOW, Marcus!" he shouted from the other end of the main corridor.

"Nah!" I said to Harj, who'd smirked at me. "It ain't funny, man. Imagine if your grandad was doin' that?" I went on.

Harj gave a shrug.

"Yeah – my grandad has got one of them 'English-Indian' accents," he told me. "It'd be well embarrassing."

"See?" I said.

"Yeah, but it ain't *my* grandad, is it?" Harj said.

"BWOI!" shouted my gramps.

"Damn! I'm gonna have to go see what he wants ..." I muttered.

I turned round and walked down the corridor. Gramps was filling in a dent in the wall. A dent that some Year Nine's head had made there.

"Easy, Gramps," I said. I was praying he was in a good mood. When he's in a bad mood even my mum stays away. And, like I said before, she's tough.

"What de problem wit' you?" he asked me.

"Huh?"

"Why you can't come chat to your gramps?" he said. At least this time I understood him.

"Er ... yeah ... I was tryin' to get to History an' that," I said.

"Only History you need to understand is that I'm your gramps," he growled. "No Gramps, no Marcus ..."

"Huh?" What was he on about?

"Bwoi – you don't understand biology?" he asked.

My head started to hurt. I stopped listening and I started to think about Mina Patel's bum instead. I knew that now I fancied her. I needed to try and get her to go out with me. I smiled to myself.

"You lose yah mind?" asked Gramps.

"Hey?"

"What you smilin' at?"

"Gotta run, Gramps," I told him.

He farted and made a kissing sound with his mouth. It wasn't to tell me he loved me. He was dissing me.

"No-good stupid boy ..." he said as I walked away. Then he farted again.

When I got back to Harj he asked me what Gramps wanted.

"Just stress, you get me?" I said. "Come on – after that I can't wait to learn about the Cold War."

The next day *was* even worse. I was walking down to Art when I saw Miss Bramley.

Now that's not a bad thing. It gives me a chance to check out her chest. But this time she was standing talking to my gramps. And that was bad news.

"I'm not sure I understand you, Mr Delgado ..." I heard her say.

"Call me Junior, sista ..." said my gramps.

There was a twinkle in his eye and he was grinning in a really cheesy way. I heard him say something else but I couldn't work out what it was. The only words I made out were 'princess' and something else that I don't wanna write in this book.

"You OK, Gramps?" I asked. I was hoping that he'd stop chatting to my teacher if I was there. Fat chance.

Gramps leaned on his mop and grinned again. He said something about an old bull and a young bull.

"Can I ask you something, miss?" I said quickly to cut Gramps off. My dad had once told me the old bull/young bull story and it was nasty.

"What do you want ...?" began Gramps.

"Sure, Marcus," said Miss Bramley. "Did I just hear you call Mr Delgado 'Gramps'?"

"Er ..." I began.

"Is he your grandad?" Miss Bramley went on.

I nodded.

"How lovely," she said, and turned to Gramps. "I didn't know Marcus was your grandson," she said to him.

Gramps made that kissing sound again. Then he said something that I couldn't understand at all. Nor could Miss Bramley. She smiled in a polite way and then said goodbye.

"Now what was it you wanted to ask me?" she said to me.

"Huh?" I replied, trying not to look too hard at her.

She looked back at me. "You said you wanted to ask me something ..."

"Oh, yeah," I said. I started to walk away from my gramps and so did she.

"So what was it?" she added.

"Er ..." I started again.

Suddenly I had an idea. "I was hoping that I could help ... you know ... at that Grand thing-y for the new library," I said without thinking.

Miss Bramley gave me a funny look.

"We'll see," she said. "Is that all you wanted?"

"Er ... yeah," I replied. "Anyway – gotta go!" I added, and walked away. Fast.

I could hear Gramps muttering as I went.

****

On the Friday of that week Gramps got a load of grief from a crew called the 2.2 Massive. I should have known they'd bother him. The 2.2 didn't like me and my mates and they wanted revenge. A month earlier me and my friends had set them up for a fall. That was why the main hall smelt so bad. They'd been picking on Harj's cousin, Kully. And we'd helped him out. Now they wanted to get us back. And everyone in school knew by then that the new caretaker was my grandad. I could smell trouble.

It was Kully who came and told me that Mitesh and the rest of the 2.2 were giving Gramps a hard time. It was lunch break and

I was with Harj checking out the girls and that. Kully ran up to us.

"They're messin' with your gramps, bro," he said to me.

"Who?" I asked.

"Mitesh and them ..." Kully panted.

"What?"

I told Kully to show me where and ran after him. Gramps was embarrassing but he was still my family and I wasn't having no stupid gangsta crew giving him grief. We ran out of the main building and down the stairs into the old school block. The building we went into was really old. The caretaker's office was down in the boiler room. I'd never been down there because pupils weren't allowed in it. As soon as we got to the top of the stairs, I heard Mitesh.

"Stupid old man ... you wanna learn to speak English, innit," Mitesh was saying.

"Yeah, man," I heard Matt Peavey say. He was another one of the 2.2 Massive.

"Leave him alone," I heard a girl say. It was Beckie, one of Kully's mates.

"Get lost, you *ho!*" shouted Mitesh.

"Who you callin' a ho?" I heard Lexie say. She was Beckie's best friend and Kully's girl.

I took the stairs in two jumps and landed right by Mitesh. He was holding a mop and swinging it around. There was water all over the floor and they'd kicked over a big bin so there was rubbish everywhere. It was a mess.

"Here comes the superhero, innit," said Dipesh. He was another member of the 2.2 Massive.

I grabbed the mop that Mitesh had in his hands and ripped it away from him. It stank. My gramps was just standing outside his office and swearing at everyone. Something in my head went 'pop!' and I smacked Mitesh in the

21

face with the mop. He cried out like a pig and then Dipesh and the others jumped me. That was when the teachers turned up.

"STOP!" boomed Mr Brimstone's voice.

We went on fighting for a moment. I had the mop-head jammed into Mitesh's face and I was rubbing it in.

"NOW!" added Brimstone.

This time everyone stopped.

"What is going on?" Mr Brimstone shouted.

"They were picking on Mr Delgado," said Lexie. "They threw all this stuff around and ..."

"No, we ain't," said Matt. "Ho be talkin' pure nonsense, you get me ..."

Kully made a jump at Matt but only made it half-way. Mr Brimstone is a big man and he almost picked Kully right up by his neck. He dragged him back.

"Mr Delgado?" asked Brimstone, as he let go of Kully as if Kully was a nasty bug.

"Me don't know who make dis mess," said my gramps really quickly. "Me just come down 'ere an' ..."

No one understood the rest of what Gramps said. Just then Mr Simms turned up as well. Right away he took the 2.2 Massive's side. But then Simms was a dick-head. He was all posh and that with the adults but when he was with Mitesh and his gang, he started talking with this stupid street accent. The nobhead.

"Did you girls see anyone do anything?" he asked.

"Er ... not exactly ..." admitted Beckie.

"So how do you know who did it?" Simms went on.

"But we ..." began Lexie.

"But nothing," said Mr Brimstone. "Everyone out of here. I'm going to talk to Mr Delgado. Go on – lunch finishes in five minutes. Upstairs now!"

I took no notice.

"You OK, Gramps?" I asked.

"Yeah, man," he said. Gramps was looking upset. He stared at all the mess he was going to have to clean up.

"You see who made the mess?" I added.

He shook his head.

"It's my job to ask the questions, boy," said Brimstone.

"But he's my ..."

"Go away right now!" Brimstone shouted.

I turned away and glared at Mitesh.

"We's gonna get you ..." Mitesh whispered.

"I'm so scared," I said. "Fire when ready ..."

"Just wait," said Mitesh. He sounded mean.

I turned to go back up the stairs with my mates.

Chapter 3
Who's Got the Goat?

Nothing happened about the mess that the 2.2 Massive made. No one saw them do it. It was left to my gramps to clean it all up. I was well angry all week-end. When Gramps came over for dinner on the Sunday I asked him about it but he just gave a shrug.

"No problem," he told me.

"But ..."

"No problem ..." he said, and then asked my dad something about the cricket.

"Ain't right," I told Harj and Kully on Monday morning.

"You wanna get back at them?" asked Kully.

I didn't know. I knew that Mitesh and his mates had done it and I wanted to get them back. But how many times can you go on? If we did something then they'd do something back. And it would just go round and round. It was stupid. What I didn't know was that something was about to happen that was going to make things a lot worse. And it was nothing to do with the 2.2 Massive.

****

It was lunch-time and me and Harj were packing our things up after a Maths lesson with Miss Bramley. Harj was talking rubbish and saying how our teacher fancied him. But he had a girlfriend and he'd been seeing her for ages. I told him so.

"What about Kelly?" I asked.

27

"I ain't sayin' I'm gonna check Bramley or nuttin'," he said. "I just know she's into me."

"How'd you know that, bro?" I wanted to know.

"It's the way she looks at me and that ..."

I shook my head. "Up until last year you were virgin bwoi and now you think you're some big-time lover-man. You wanna be careful ..."

"Leave it, Marcus, man. Just 'cos she likes me," Harj said.

"I don't think so, bro. She must have a man anyways ..."

"Why?" asked Harj.

"'Cos she's *fit*, bro, you get me? No way a woman like that ain't got a man ..."

"You two are like little puppies," said Lucy from behind us. "It's pathetic."

"Woof woof!" I replied.

We walked down the stairs and into the main corridor where a load of teachers were standing around. Mr Brimstone and Mrs Pincher looked grim.

"Summat's going on," Harj said to me.

"Huh?"

"Check them teachers, bro. Summat is up," Harj said.

I looked at Brimstone. His face was all red and there were sweat patches in his armpits. Like he'd been running around. I wanted to walk up to him and say 'deodorant' but I didn't. Instead I looked at the rest of the teachers. They all looked upset.

"You're right, Harj. Something's happened," I said.

A bit later we were finishing our dinners when Lexie and Beckie showed up with Ben, another one of their friends.

"You heard the news?" asked Ben, with a grin.

"Nah – what's up?" I said.

"Flossie's done a runner," he told me. He was trying not to laugh.

"*Flossie?*" I asked. "Who's Flossie?"

"Flossie the goat, bro," Harj said.

"Oh, no ..."

That was what Brimstone had been fretting about. And sweating too.

"They've had *all* the Year Sevens out looking for it," added Lexie. "No one can find it."

"Maybe it's gone into town," Harj laughed. "Gone to get its hair done for the Grand Opening ..."

"It ain't funny," said Beckie. "Brimstone and Pincher are going mad. I heard Simms say that there's gonna be big trouble ..."

I gave a shrug. "Over a goat?" I asked.

Lexie and Beckie nodded together as Kully walked up.

"It's *only* a goat," I added. What was all the fuss was about?

"It's not just any old goat," said Ben. "It's the school mascot, remember?"

"It's a stinky, hairy, smelly old goat," said Harj. "Ain't no one bothered if it's gone missing."

Kully looked away for a moment. He hated the goat. But maybe you know that from another story.

31

"It's *you*, innit?" I said to Kully. "You kidnapped it?"

Lexie grinned. "You should really say '*goat*-napped'," she said.

"Huh?" asked Harj, dim as ever.

"Well, if it's a baby goat then *kid*-napped works but ..."

Harj looked at me.

"What you bangin' on about, you nutter?"

"Er ... it's a *joke?*" Beckie said. "A baby goat is called a 'kid', you div ..."

"Oh," said Harj. "Still ain't funny."

"Well, it's not as funny as your dress sense," Lexie said.

"Or your haircut," added Beckie.

"Or the way you walk like your shoes are too small," Lexie went on.

The rest of us started to laugh as Harj went red.

"Poor Flossie," said Lexie. "Out there all on her own. What if she's scared? What if she's been taken by aliens? It happens to humans all the time so I don't see why it can't happen to a goat too ..."

I looked at Lexie and then at Kully.

"She *always* that crazy, bro?" I asked him.

"Nah," he told me. "She's being good today ..."

"Lexie's right," said Beckie. "What if Flossie got out and a bus ran her over?"

"Then we'll be havin' goat curry for lunch tomorrow," I said.

That was a joke. But jokes can come back to haunt you. That one did.

It was three days later when things really kicked off. In the morning we had another full school Assembly and Mr Brimstone was well upset.

"You'll know by now, I'm sure, that Flossie has gone missing," he said. "Terrible news ... terrible ..."

For a moment he lost it and couldn't say anything. I turned to Harj and grinned.

"My man's lost it now," I said.

Harj shook his head.

"Over a goat ... that's just weird, bro," he replied.

Mr Brimstone waited a moment to calm himself down and then went on.

"Now some of you may not think this is important. But that goat is part of this school. She's one of our own *family* and she's gone missing. We must do all in our power to get her back."

I looked around to see if anyone else thought he was crazy too. But some of my fellow pupils were as mad as he was. Harriet, a girl in my form, was sobbing, and another girl, Lisa, had a 'Find Our Flossie' badge. For a minute I thought I'd slipped into a parallel universe but then Harj started to cough so as to stop himself laughing.

"This is so stupid," I said.

Harriet turned and gave me an evil look. I ignored her. Brimstone started banging on about the local newspapers and how the goat was so important for the day we opened the new library. The whole world was going mad. And it was about to get madder. As we all went back out of the hall to go to lessons, some Year Sevens were handing out home-made badges, posters and stickers.

"Help find our Flossie," one of them said to me. "Ask your neighbours to look and put a sticker in your front window ... **Find our Flossie.**"

"It's in the bathroom cabinet," Harj told him. "Next to the toothpaste."

"That's not funny, Harj," said Harriet from behind us. "Flossie is one of us ..."

"Are you mental?" I asked her.

But Harriet just ignored me and walked off with her friends. Snooty moose.

****

I didn't think it was a big problem until that lunch-time. That's when I *had* to get involved in the search for Flossie. I didn't have a choice. I was trying to chat up Mina Patel when Lexie and Kully found me.

"It's your grandad," said Lexie.

"What about him?" I asked.

"Someone saw him take the goat and now he's eating goat curry ..."

My head began to spin.

"*Goat* curry?" I couldn't believe it.

"Yeah," said Kully. "There was this smell coming from the boiler room and when Mr Simms went down there he found your gramps eating goat curry."

"*No!*"

Lexie nodded.

"Pincher and Brimstone are with him now. Asking him lots of questions ..."

"How'd you know that?" I wanted to know.

"We just saw him being led into Pincher's office ... it looked bad."

"Did Gramps say anything?" I asked.

"Just something we couldn't understand about hands and blood ..."

"Huh?" I couldn't work it out.

Kully put his hand on my arm.

"It's looking bad, bro. First the goat goes missing and then your grandad starts eating goat curry. I ain't no detective but something ain't right ..."

I stood where I was. What was I going to do? There was no way my gramps would have killed Flossie. Was there?

Chapter 4
A Confession

In the end my dad came into school to help Gramps but it was no good. Mrs Pincher and Mr Brimstone were mad with anger, Dad told me. They kept on talking about how important Flossie was. How the school'd look silly if Flossie wasn't at the Grand Opening because they'd told the local newspapers all about her.

"But me never touch de goat," Gramps kept saying.

Brimstone didn't believe him. He told Gramps that he couldn't work at the school until they'd found out what had happened.

"But you don't have any proof that my father took the goat," my dad said to Mrs Pitcher and Mr Brimstone.

"I'm afraid we do, Mr Delgado," Mrs Pincher said. "Some pupils saw your father take it."

"Pupils?" asked Dad.

"Yes. They say they saw Mr Delgado with Flossie on the night she went missing."

"But that was days ago," my dad said. "Why didn't they say anything sooner?"

Brimstone gave a cough and Pincher looked at Dad. "They said that your father told them he'd make them into curry too ..."

"Never!" said Dad. "That's just stupid. Why would he do that?"

Dad said Gramps just sat where he was and said nothing. He kept shaking his head and saying he was innocent, that he'd been set up by 'de Massive dem'. That was when it clicked.

It was Mitesh and his mates who'd set up Gramps. Had to be.

"Why would they do that?" Dad asked me when we got home after school.

"Because they've got a problem with me and my mates," I had to admit.

Dad gave me a stern look.

"What beef, Marcus?"

"Nothing really ... we just had some trouble with them and they want revenge. That's why they've picked on Gramps."

Dad shook his head.

"So your gramps might lose his job and all the teachers are upset. And all because you got some argument going on?"

"Looks like it," I nodded.

"Well, I hope for your sake that he gets his job back. He was very upset when I dropped him at his flat."

"I'm sorry, Dad, but it's not our fault. It's the 2.2 Massive."

Dad shook his head.

"Since your grandma died, your gramps has been really lonely and down. That job was his way of getting over it. And now it's gone because of one of your arguments and some bloody stupid goat."

You know how parents have a way of making you feel about three years old even when you're a teenager? That's how I felt. I felt terrible. And I hadn't even done anything. Once Dad had stopped making me feel bad I got right on the phone to Harj.

"Summat ain't right," I told him.

Harj laughed on the other end of the line.

"Yeah – but I bet that curry tasted good. You could smell it all over the school, bro," he joked.

"It ain't no joke, Harj. My gramps is being set up by the 2.2 Massive and we've gotta do summat about it."

"What?" Harj didn't understand me.

I thought about it for a moment. "I dunno," I said in the end. "But I helped you and Kully out and now you need to help me ..."

"Just say the word, bro," replied Harj. "We got yer back ..."

****

I had to wait until after the week-end to see Mitesh. He was kicking a ball around outside school with Matt and Jitinder. I was so angry when I saw him that I didn't care that I was on my own. I wasn't bothered. I just wanted to get to him. I walked up to Mitesh but he didn't see me coming. He lost the ball, turned to see where it had gone and saw me standing right behind him. I kicked the ball away and came up close to him.

"Whad d'ya want?" Mitesh asked.

"I wanna know why you're telling lies about my grandad," I told him.

He gave a nasty grin. "Dunno what you're on about ..."

"The goat," I went on. "You told Brimstone that you seen my gramps take the goat."

"Maybe," Mitesh replied.

He was trying to act cool but I could see in his piggy eyes that I was right. Mitesh and his gang *had* gone to Brimstone and told him that stupid story about Gramps.

"Well, you need to go and tell Brimstone that you were wrong," I said.

"Or what?" asked Jitinder, getting all mean-looking.

"Or nuttin'," I replied. "I ain't getting into a fight with you. I'm just saying. Sort it out ..."

This time it was Jitinder who grinned back at me.

"What you gonna do if we don't?" he asked me again.

"Depends," I said. "You go tell Brimstone that you were wrong and nothing. You don't admit you lied – then we got problems."

Matt Peavey started to laugh so I grabbed his nose between my fingers and twisted it.

"OWW!" he squealed, just like a little girl.

"Back off!" shouted Jitinder. "There's three of us and one of you ..."

"That's about equal, then," I said with a smile.

45

"Just get lost," said Mitesh. "We definitely seen your grandad take the goat and we ain't sayin' no different. You get me?"

My smile vanished.

"I got you," I told him. "You got a problem with me – fine. But that's an old man you're messing with. Ain't you got no shame?"

"Nah," replied Mitesh. "Anyway – he was on at us too. Said he'd make us into curry ..."

"It don't matter how many times you lie," I told him. "It ain't gonna turn into the truth just 'cos you keep saying it ..."

"It ain't no lie," said Jitinder.

I thought about hitting him but changed my mind. I don't know what I'd thought was going to happen when I went up to them. It wasn't like they were going to help me, was it? I was going to have to find some other way of helping Gramps out. I looked back at Jitinder.

"You heard what I said," I told him. "You do something or I'll go to Miss Bramley and tell her how you get your sister to do all your homework, innit."

Jitinder's face went bright red and I walked off into school.

****

That night I went round to see my gramps at his flat. He growled at me when he opened the door and I followed him in without a word. The living room was full of pictures. They were everywhere and they were really dusty. There were pictures of me and Teesha and my old man from when he was younger. And there were loads of pictures of us with Mum, all smiling and laughing and that. But mostly the pictures were of my gran.

"You OK, Gramps?" I asked, as I sat down on a sofa that was older than I was.

Gramps gave a shrug.

"What you been doin'?" I added.

He said something I didn't understand.

"I'm sorry about what happened to you," I said, trying to smile.

"S'alright," he replied. "It's nah your fault, bwoi."

"The 2.2 Massive only picked on you because I've got a problem with them," I told him.

"Still not your fault," he said.

"Have you heard from the school?"

"Yeah, man ... dem say something about me wait for my job an' all that ..." Gramps said.

"So what *did* happen, then?" I asked.

"Nuttin'. Me just sittin' at work, eating me curry and dem say me kill dem goat ..."

"But you didn't kill the goat, did you?" I said. I was hoping ... Praying ...

"Why would I wan' kill dem goat?" Gramps asked. "An' lose a perfectly good job? Me ain't that stupid, Marcus."

I smiled at him. It was stupid of me to even think that he'd killed Flossie. There were *much* simpler ways to get goat curry.

"So when Mitesh and them say they seen you take the goat – they was lying ..." I tried again.

He looked over at a picture of my gran.

"Marcus?" he said after a bit.

"Yes, Gramps?"

"You know how me never lie to you ...?"

My heart sank and my stomach turned over.

"Er ... yeah?" I said slowly. I had this funny feeling.

49

"Me might just have tek de blasted goat ..." he whispered.

"Huh?"

"Me say me tek de blasted goat – yuh deaf bwoi?" he shouted.

My mouth fell open. I started to sweat. My stomach felt like the inside of a washing machine.

"You *took* it?" I gasped.

"Yeah, man," he admitted.

"But you *didn't* kill it ...?"

"Yeah, man ..."

I looked at him and shook my head. I didn't understand. "What – you didn't kill it or you *did*?"

He looked back at me and gave a shrug.

"Me never kill it," he told me.

Thank God for that, I thought.

"Me friend at de butchers – him kill it for me ..." Gramps went on.

I couldn't believe what I was hearing.

"So let me get this right, Gramps," I said slowly. "You *did* take Flossie and you *did* have her killed. And you *were* eating her in school?"

"Yes, man!" he said. He sounded put out by my questions.

"Why?" I had to know.

"What else was I gonna do, bwoi?"

"Er ... you *could* have left it alone, Gramps," I said. "Just got on with your job and ignored it ..."

"*Ignore* it? All day long de thing just *bleat bleat bleat*. Me can't even sleep at night – all me hear is de blasted *goat*."

"Oh my God ..." I added. The 2.2 Massive had been right. And I'd gone for them. Now they'd want to get me back.

"And too," said Gramps. "De *raasclaat* thing shit pon me clean floor ..."

My heart sank down to somewhere near my knees.

"Oh, no ..." I heard myself say.

Chapter 5
Lexie's Plan

I spent the night worrying about what Gramps had said. I couldn't believe that he'd taken Flossie. He'd had her killed and eaten her. It was crazy. I mean, what did he think he was doing? Now what was I going to do? Was I going to tell my parents? Or was I going to help my Gramps out of a hole? My head was spinning.

In the morning I grabbed Harj. I looked around to check no one could hear me. There were some Year Eights hanging around and I told them to get lost.

"Got a serious problem, bro," I told Harj. "Serious ..."

"Yeah," joked Harj. "Your B.O. and your nasty breath. I know ..."

"No time for jokes, bro. I need your help," I went on.

"Is this about your gramps?" asked Harj.

"Yeah."

Harj gave a sigh. "I dunno what we can do, bro."

I gulped. I needed to tell him the truth but I didn't want to. In the end I knew I had no choice.

"Gramps took Flossie," I whispered.

"You're joking!" shouted Harj.

"Ssshhhh!" I begged.

"But ..." Harj looked so shocked.

"Just shut up, Harj, and listen ..."

"But ..." he began.

"He took it, had it killed and ate it, bro," I said. "He told me ..."

Harj started to shake his head.

"Yeah, I know – I was shocked too but what can I do?" I said

Suddenly Harj started to laugh. Loud.

"Shut up, bro ..." I said over and over but it was no use. Harj was having fits.

"That's the funniest thing I've heard. Ever!" he said.

"It ain't funny, Harj. It's serious ..."

He shook his head and tried to say something in between the laughter.

"*Funny* ..." he squealed. His face was going red and tears were rolling down his cheeks. "*Ate ... the ... goat!*"

"What are we gonna do, bro?" I said again.

"Ask him for a taste ..." said Harj.

There was no way he was going to be serious. He was having too much fun laughing. But it really wasn't funny. I was stuck. It was my gramps after all. And right or wrong, I wanted to help him out.

"What do they do in them police shows on the telly ..." I started to say.

That made Harj laugh even harder. "Tests, bro," he giggled. "Maybe we could get a poo sample from your grandad and check for goat DNA?"

"Harj!" I shouted.

But it was no good. Harj went on talking about it for the rest of the day. Every time we were on our own. It didn't help that Mr Brimstone was walking around the school with a face like thunder. It was like someone had killed a member of his family. It was nuts.

And on every corner there were **Find Our Flossie** posters. I couldn't get away from that damn goat. Even thinking about Mina's bum didn't help. I was going crazy. I couldn't let my gramps take the fall. Even if he *had* done it. I mean, it wasn't his fault. When he was a kid in Jamaica, maybe people ate goats all the time. It was no big thing for him.

I got all of my mates to meet at Lexie's house that evening. Maybe they'd help me.

"What's going on?" Ben asked.

"Later," I said. "But it's serious."

****

Lexie's parents were working late so no worries from them. I was the first to get to Lexie's house and I had to wait around outside for the others. One of Lexie's next-door-neighbours came out and asked what I was doing.

"Sitting on a wall," I told her. The nosy old bag.

"Do you know the family who live here?" she asked.

"Er ... no. That's why I'm outside their house waiting for them to come home. Innit?"

The woman gave me a dirty look and hobbled off back into her house. Just then Lexie turned up with Kully, Ben and Beckie.

"Wow!" said Beckie. "You're keen. What's so important?"

"I'll tell you inside," I said.

Harj arrived fifteen minutes later with his girlfriend. "You're late, bro," I said.

"Relax, Marcus," he replied. "Anyone would think you'd eaten something funny. Your face is green ..."

I swore at him and told the rest of them to sit down.

"It's about Flossie," I said. It was better to get to the point quickly.

Five minutes later everyone was sitting staring at me like I had mushrooms growing out of my head. Dancing and singing mushrooms.

"Are you out of your tiny little mind?" asked Beckie. "I mean, I know it's small but please ..."

"You on about his mind or his willy?" Ben joked.

"This is serious ..." I said. It felt like I'd been saying that all day.

"No, it's just stupid," replied Kully. "Your gramps ate Flossie and that's it. Ain't nothing we can do about it ..."

"But there *has* to be summat," I said. "When Harj needed help I was there. And when Kully had his trouble with the 2.2 Massive I was there too ..."

Harj snorted.

"But that wasn't about your gramps killing and eating the school mascot. I mean, he didn't even share ..."

"So what – now I'm in trouble none of you want to help?" I asked. I felt really let down.

"We didn't say that," all the girls said at the same time.

"Man, you lot are like them identical twins," said Kully to the girls.

"Apart from the fact that we don't look the same and we ain't related?" asked Lexie.

"Yeah – other than those two little things – we could be triplets," added Beckie.

"Piglets more like," said Ben.

"**Stop!**" shouted Harj's girlfriend.

Everyone did as they were told and turned to her. She was grinning like a mad woman.

"What?" I asked.

"I've got the seed of an idea," she said. "Only it's gonna take some planning ..."

"Do *we* have to do anything illegal?" asked Harj.

"Not really, no," she told him.

"Not really?"

She shook her head.

"Trust me, young man. I'm gonna need the girls for this, so lads – get lost and let us think ..." she ordered.

"But why can't we stay and ..." I began.

"**Shoo!**" she said. "Now would be good ..."

I got up slowly.

"We've got football practice anyway," Harj said. "Come on ..."

I was rubbish at football practice. I couldn't have hit a cow's bum with a frying pan. Never mind score a goal. As soon as we'd finished I rang the girls. I wanted to know what they'd come up with. But none of them answered their phones. I was going mad. What were they doing?

"Relax," Harj told me on the way home. "Tell me about that Mina Patel. You and her on yet or what?"

I shook my head.

"She's thinking about it," I told him, but I wasn't really thinking about what he'd asked. All I could think about was goats.

"Thinking about it?" he asked.

"Yeah ..."

"But you're the only one out of us who ain't hooked up," he reminded me. "I'm with Kelly, Lexie and Kully are going out and even Ben and Beckie are bumpin' uglies ..."

"So?" I asked, as Flossie's face came up in my head again.

"So you need to catch some action too, bro ..." Harj went on.

I wasn't really listening. I had Flossie's voice in my ear.

"*Baaad, baaad, baaad,*" she bleated.

A shiver ran down my spine.

Chapter 6
The Plan in Action

Lexie and Beckie didn't come into school the next day. Both of them had called in sick. And when I asked Harj to ring Kelly, who went to different school, he got no reply.

"Funny, that," he said when she didn't ring him back at lunch-time. "She always rings back."

"Something funny's going on," I said.

"What – funnier than your gramps eating Flossie?"

"Shut up!" I shouted, just as Miss Bramley walked past us in the corridor.

"Something wrong, boys?" she asked with a smile. She was *soooo* fit.

Harj went red and his mouth fell wide open so I had to do the talking.

"It's nothing, miss ..." I said, trying to stay cool. She smelled like flowers and sweets.

"Good," she said. Then she went on, "By the way you'll both be helping with the Grand Opening on Friday. There's a meeting about it at morning break tomorrow."

"*Huh?*" I asked. I wasn't really listening.

"The library *opening*? You asked me about it when I was talking to your *grandad*?" she said.

"Oh, yeah," I remembered now. "Is that *this* week?"

"Yes," she replied. "It's just such a shame that Flossie's still lost and then there's all that awful stuff with Mr Delgado. How is he, by the way?"

I looked at Harj but he had his mouth open as if he'd been turned into a zombie. So I looked at the floor.

"He's OK," I said. "Bit down and that ..."

When I looked up, Miss Bramley was nodding as if she felt really sorry for Gramps.

"I just can't see how your grandad would do such a nasty thing," she told me. "I know what those lads said but I can't believe it. He's *such* a sweet old man ..."

"Sweet like goat meat," Harj muttered very softly.

"I'm sorry?" Miss Bramley asked.

"Er ... I said ... er ... toilet seat!" Harj blurted out quickly.

I gave him a death stare. What the hell was he on about?

"*Toilet* seat?" asked Miss Bramley, looking puzzled and fit at the same time.

"Er, yeah," said Harj.

I knew he was making up a story in his head. I could see he was thinking hard. His eyes were all blank and that. Here was my chance to get him back for all the dodgy jokes about my gramps and Flossie.

"Tell miss about the toilet seat, Harj," I said. "Go on ..."

"I ... er ... *broke* it this morning and I have to get a new one before my dad finds out," he said quickly.

"I see," said Miss Bramley, looking at Harj in an odd way. Then she smiled at him so sweetly.

"Do you know where I can get one?" he added, much more slowly. I could see he was proud that he could make something up so quickly.

Miss Bramley looked at me. It was an *'is he for real?'* sort of look.

"Try the big DIY store on the ring road," she said.

"Thanks, miss. You're really great!" Harj said, getting as cheesy as a Wotsit.

"Will you both come to the meeting tomorrow?" she asked.

"Yes, miss," I said.

"Good. I'll see you in Maths later." And with that she walked off. Harj stood and stared after her.

"She's *so* fit!" he said. "I swear she wants me, bro. See how she always stops to chat when I'm around? I'm tellin' you ..."

"Shut up, Harj," I said. My mind was working overtime now. It was Tuesday and we didn't have much time left. We had to do something before Friday. Something to help my gramps. But what? And where the hell were the girls?

****

Lexie rang me at six o'clock that evening.

"Where have you been all day?" I asked.

"Busy ... I need you to meet me and the others in an hour," she said.

"Why?"

"Never mind about that," Lexie told me. "Do you want to help your gramps or not?"

"Yeah," I said.

"And tell your parents you're going out or something. It could be a late night ..." she added.

"How late?" I asked.

"Depends," she said. "See you at seven ..."

"But ..." I began, only she'd gone.

My dad was sitting watching telly. There was a news story on about some politician and he was well into it.

"I'm ... er ... goin' to this thing later, Dad," I said.

"Yeah," he replied. He didn't even turn round to look at me – his attention was on the TV.

"Might get back a bit late and that ..." I tried again.

"Yeah," Dad said.

"What you watching?" I asked.

"Yeah," he said for the third time.

This was my chance to go.

"OK then – I'll ring if it gets too late ..."

My dad looked up at me, nodded and then went back to watching the news. Result!

****

Lexie's parents weren't home when I got there. They had gone away for a few days. Her older sister, Lilly, had been left in charge.

"But she's out with her mates," Lexie told me. "Besides, Mum and Dad won't call. They're in Venice."

"Nice. So what are we doin'?" I asked.

"Going to find Flossie," she told me, with a wink.

"But Flossie's dead ..." I pointed out.

"All in good time, Marcus ..." Lexie said.

Kelly, Harj and Kully turned up five minutes later.

"Let's go," said Harj as soon as they arrived.

"Where we going?" I asked.

Harj walked out of the house and I followed him. Everyone else came too. He pointed at a tatty old white van.

"In there," he said, pointing at it.

"What the hell ...?" I began to say as I looked at the van. It was junk.

That was when Beckie's big sister stuck her head out of the van window.

"Hurry up!" she ordered.

"But why are you helping us?" I asked.

"She owes me," Beckie told me. "Don't worry – she'll keep our secret and she won't tell."

I looked at Harj and Kelly. They both gave me a shrug.

"It's *something*, isn't it?" said Kelly.

"Er … yeah," I said. "It's a rusty old van with a kid driving it. Where are we going?"

"Come on!" Beckie shouted. "We borrowed this from my dad's yard and it's got to go back tonight …"

Beckie's dad, Mr Clapper, was a builder. What would he do if he found out that Beckie had taken one of his vans? As I got into the back I asked her.

"He won't do anything," Beckie told me. "It's my mum I've got to worry about."

But that didn't help. Things were just getting more and more weird.

****

Beckie's sister drove us out of the city and into the countryside. We'd been going for about 20 minutes before she stopped. Because I was in the back, I didn't see where she'd stopped. And by now it was dark. Beckie jumped out of the front of the van with Kelly and they let the rest of us out of the back. The smell hit me straight away. It was a nasty, thick farm smell.

I jumped out into almost pitch darkness. I asked Beckie where we were.

"A farm," I heard Kelly say from somewhere to my side.

Harj and Kully turned on torches and at last I saw where we were. There was a long metal gate in front of us. Beyond the gate were three big barns that loomed out of the dark like monsters.

"What are we doin' at a farm?" I asked.

"Looking for Flossie's twin ..." said Harj.

"Are you goin' mental, bro?" I said.

"Nope," he replied.

"What are we going to do – just walk in and take a goat?" I added.

"Yes," said Kelly. "That's exactly what we're going to do ..."

"But isn't that illegal – like theft?" asked Lexie.

"Maybe," replied Kully.

"But unless you've got a better idea," Beckie added, "it's time to go and get us a new Flossie ..."

I looked around at my mad friends and I shook my head. What was this crazy let's-go-steal-a-random-goat idea about? Part of me was shocked. But then another part of me thought this was well funny. We were cattle thieves, rustlers, like in those cowboy movies my gramps likes. Only we were after a goat and not cows.

"So how do you know this farm even *has* goats?" I asked Kelly.

75

"Been here for a school thing," she told me. "And when Ben called us piglets the other day it just clicked ... they make goat's cheese here. All three barns are full of goats. There are loads of them."

"It's like 'Goats R Us'," Harj joked.

"Goat City," added Lexie.

"Goat World," said Beckie, killing the joke dead.

Kully opened the gate and we walked in. The track we were walking along was made of dried mud. There were huge ruts in it and my feet slipped a couple of times.

"I'm gonna break my ankle out here!" I said.

"**Sssshhh!!!!!!!!**" whispered Lexie. "Do you want us to get caught?"

"Yeah, bro," added Kully. "These farmers carry guns and that ..."

"*Big* guns," said Harj.

But we didn't come across any mad farmers with shot-guns. In fact, it was really easy to get to the barns. And the doors weren't even locked.

"Silly farmer ..." said Kully, as we stepped inside the first barn.

Harj and Kully shone their torches around. Kelly and Beckie pulled out torches too and turned them on. As they did so, I saw *goats*. Lots and lots of *goats*. And they saw us too. Black eye-balls glinted in the light of the torches. Voices began to bleat.

"Pick a goat," said Kelly. "Any goat ..."

Chapter 7
Cut a Long Story Short

Whenever my sister tells a story about anything my dad always says, "Cut a long story short." And that's what I'm going to do. I could tell you all about the goat we 'borrowed'. How she looked just like Flossie, right down to the evil stare and razor-sharp horns. How we had to catch her because she ran away. How she butted Kully and sent Lexie falling into a pile of poo. Then there was all the trouble it took to get her into the van, get her back to the city and hide her in Lexie's garage. But I'm not gonna do that.

To cut a long story short, by the morning of the Grand Opening of the new library, we had 'Flossie' hidden in the boiler room, tied to a water pipe. Waiting. As me and Harj were helping with the Opening, we couldn't check that no one saw 'Flossie' before it was time. So Lexie and Beckie had to hang around the old school building and see that no one went into the boiler room. But that was easy. Because the school was full of boring old 'important' people like the Mayor and the local MP. None of the kids in the Lower School were around because they'd been given the day off. Ben and Kully were helping the girls, looking out for anything that might be a problem. The rest of the school was busy getting ready for a special Assembly. And that was in the main building.

Mrs Pincher and Mr Simms were running around like nutcases, to make sure everything ran smoothly. Mr Brimstone was really calm. Instead of being his normal frantic self, he looked sad.

"He's missin' Flossie," said Harj, when we saw him in the main corridor.

"Well, he's in for a shock, innit?" I said.

"Too right. It's a good job I found her twin for you," boasted Harj. It had been Harj who'd spotted 'Flossie' in the barn and he'd been banging on about how great he was ever since.

"Alright, alright," I told him, "don't get all high and mighty about it."

"Just sayin' – that's all," he said. "It's a good job I checked that goat over ... no one is going to spot the difference."

"I hope not ..." I told him. "Otherwise we're in trouble ..."

As we chatted, Mr Brimstone walked past us like we didn't even exist. You could see in his eyes that he was upset. It was like he was just staring at nothing all the time. It was weird.

"You OK, sir?" I asked.

But he didn't answer. Instead it was Miss Bramley who stopped to talk. Again. Harj shot it straight away. His went all glassy and his mouth fell open.

"Hi, miss," he said.

"Hi, Harj ... is Mr Brimstone OK?" asked Miss Bramley.

I shook my head. "I think he's missing his goat," I said.

"Poor man – that goat was like his pet," Miss Bramley told us. "Ever since his wife left him ..."

I gulped down air. I was already feeling bad but now it was even worse. The guilt was hanging around my neck like a big snake, a boa constrictor, squashing the air out of my lungs.

"Are you OK, Marcus?" asked Miss Bramley. She looked really worried.

I nodded and tried to breathe properly.

"Yeah – just this thing I got ..." I began.

"I got a thing too ..." muttered Harj. "Special ting for miss ..."

"Excuse me?" asked Miss Bramley.

"Oh, nothing, miss," said Harj, just as Mr Simms walked over to us.

Simms is one of them teachers who think it's cool to talk like the kids. It'd be OK if he really did talk like that but he doesn't. He just puts it on.

"Yes, my bros," he said to me and Harj. But he wasn't looking at us. He was eyeing up Miss Bramley. Like a rat.

"Yeah," I said.

"Miss Bramley ..." Simms went on. He was cheesier than a ton of Red Leicester.

"Er ... yeah," said Miss Bramley. She looked uncomfy and her cheeks went a dark pink colour.

"Lotta work to do, my boss, you get me?" Mr Simms said to me. Something flew out of his mouth and past my head. "Best you just go away. Innit?"

That was when I clicked. Mr Simms was trying to get rid of me and Harj so that he could be on his own with Miss Bramley. I looked at my best mate. He looked back at me. He knew what I knew. And we both knew that Miss Bramley didn't like him. We couldn't leave him alone with her. It would be rude.

"Did you say you wanted to show us something, miss?" I asked.

For a moment I thought she wouldn't understand but she did. She nodded.

"Er ... yes," she said. "You need to come to my office, lads ..."

"What's *this?*" asked Mr Simms. You could see in his face that he was pissed off. Jealous even. You could also see bits of something green stuck in his teeth. The man was a scutter.

"Er ... miss needs some help with her computer," said Harj quickly.

"I can help you with that," Mr Simms said to Miss Bramley, spitting all over her. She stepped back.

"Nah – it's one of them Facebook-type things," I added. "*You* wouldn't get it ..."

Simms gave us both a dirty look.

"Come on, lads," said Miss Bramley. "Before things get ... *er* ... busy ..."

She turned and walked towards the stairs which led to the Maths classrooms.

Mr Simms just stood and looked at me. I turned and went off with Harj, who was walking behind Miss Bramley, up the stairs. When we got to Miss Bramley's office she gave us both a big grin.

"Thanks, lads!" she beamed. "You're real gentlemen," she told us.

And with that she went into her office and closed the door. We stayed in the corridor, looking at each other. Our mouths opened and closed but nothing came out. We looked like fish out of water, panting for air ...

****

It was in the special Assembly that we were going to let 'Flossie' out. After all the stuff with Mr Simms and Miss Bramley, Harj and I nearly forgot about our plan. It was Beckie who found us. We were sitting on the floor in the Maths corridor, staring into space.

"What the hell happened to you two?" she asked when she saw us.

"Heaven ..." whispered Harj.

"You what?" said Beckie. "You gone nuts?"

"No ..." added Harj, smiling like a madman.

Beckie gave me a funny look.

"What?" I asked.

"Just the small matter of a *goat?*" she said.

We ran past the main hall and around it to a corridor at the back. The corridor led to the PE block. Lexie and Kully were down there, in the girls' changing rooms, waiting with 'Flossie'. They'd waited until everyone was in the main hall and then dragged the goat around the outside of the building and in through a fire door. The plan was to wait until the Assembly had started and Mr Brimstone was talking. Beckie ran and stood outside the changing room door. I stood halfway down the corridor. Harj took up position at the top, behind the doors into the main hall. He was peering through a gap in the curtains on the door, waiting for Brimstone to start. And Ben was in the hall, ready to make excuses in case anyone noticed that we were missing.

We only had to wait a few minutes when Harj nodded at me. I turned and nodded at Beckie. She put her thumb up and opened the door to the changing room. I heard Kully swear and then he dragged the goat out on the end of some rope. Lexie was behind the goat, trying to push it. 'Flossie' didn't want to move. In the end Beckie had to pull a random drawing pin off a display board and stick it in the goat's arse. 'Flossie's' eyes sparked and she charged up the corridor, dragging Kully with her. When she got to Harj, he opened the door and the goat charged into the middle of the Assembly, with the rest of us right behind her.

The whole room stopped and gasped. Someone shouted 'Flossie!' I looked around at the crowd. The faces were full of shock. The faces of the 2.2 Massive were worst of all.

"Nah, bro!" shouted Mitesh. "We seen him take it. We *seen* it!"

And then everyone started to cheer and shout and whoop. 'Flossie' just ran around trying to butt people. Kully tried to control her but she wasn't having it. She ran straight at Mr Simms and shoved her head into his privates. He squealed and fell to the floor. That led to even more cheers and howls of laughter. That was when 'Flossie' started to chase the Lord Mayor. I span round to see what Mr Brimstone was doing. He was standing at the microphone, staring at the goat. It seemed like a long time before he did anything. But when he did, he was fast. He grabbed the goat by the horns and dragged it to the front of the hall. The Lord Mayor stopped running and started to straighten out his clothes. His face was beetroot red.

Harj poked me in the ribs.

"Check out Brimstone, bro …" he said.

I turned to see Brimstone. He was down by the goat, stroking it. There was silence as everyone looked over.

"Flossie …" said Brimstone, with tears in his eyes. "I thought you were dead …"

He was like a small child and I thought he was going to start sobbing and that. But he didn't. Instead he stopped suddenly, stood up and looked at me and my mates.

"*This* isn't Flossie," he said softly …

"HUH?" we all said together.

"This isn't Flossie …" he said again, louder this time.

I looked at the goat and saw what Brimstone was on about. I turned to Harj.

"You *stupid, thick, pea-brained fool*," I said, "Checked it over, yeah?"

"What?" he asked, looking very puzzled.

Mr Brimstone's face was turning redder and redder.

"This isn't *Flossie*," he boomed at us, "because **Flossie didn't have a willy!!!**"

Harj's face fell.

"Oops ..." he muttered.

"We're dead," I added ...

Barrington Stoke would like to thank all its readers for commenting on the manuscript before publication and in particular:

Noureena Ali

Jade Creighton

Leanne Devlin

Natasha Farrington

Ashley Hayes

Miss Heywood

Luke Hoskisson

Jessica Kelleher

Kyle Sheperdson

Sarah Walters

Become a Consultant!

Would you like to give us feedback on our titles before they are published? Contact us at the email address below – we'd love to hear from you!

info@barringtonstoke.co.uk
www.barringtonstoke.co.uk

Great reads – no problem!

Barrington Stoke books are:

Great stories – from thrillers to comedy to horror, and all by the best writers around!

No hassle – fast reads with no boring bits, and a story that doesn't let go of you till the last page.

Short – the perfect size for a fast, fun read.

We use our own font and paper to make it easier to read our books. And we ask teenagers like you, who want a no-hassle read, to check every book before it's published.

That way, we know for sure that every Barrington Stoke book is a great read for everyone.

Check out <u>www.barringtonstoke.co.uk</u> for more info about Barrington Stoke and our books!

Two-Timer

Harj has no girlfriend and no hope, as his friends keep telling him. So when not one but two of the fittest girls in town ask him out how can he say no? At first he feels bad about cheating ... then he starts to enjoy it! But how long can he play this game?

Revenge of the Number Two

Life at school's never easy but for Kully there's no hope. His school life has gone down the toilet – all because he didn't go. To the toilet. Will Kully always be "Mr Number Two"? Or can he get his revenge on the bullies who make his life a misery? The hilarious gross-out sequel to *Two-Timer*.

You can order these books directly from our website at
www.barringtonstoke.co.uk

Dream On

Baljit's mates know what's what. If you are good at football, really good, you can go places. But all his old man ever talks about is duty to the family and paying bills. Baljit can't keep going on working in his old man's chippie. He wants out!

What's Your Problem?

Jaspal is a city boy and life in a village just isn't for him. Moreover, he's the only Asian teenager around. When the insults begin, Jaspal's dad tells him that things will be OK – but the racism gets worse. Soon it becomes clear that things will never get better. Jaspal's life will never be the same again ...

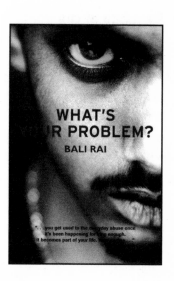

You can order these books directly from our website at
www.barringtonstoke.co.uk